Toni & Lorenza

A/N: An unlikely partnership and an unlikely love. Anyone who likes gangster, criminal or downright awesome action fury should love this story if it turns out as I hope it will. There's crime, friendship, romance and action in this story.

Chapter 1: The Beginning At The End

Two girls with black hair were running away from cops in an airport. One was wearing a black tank-top and brown denim jeans with black and white converses and her hair was in a messy ponytail. The other was wearing a black tank top with black denim jeans and black and white converse and her hair was long and straight with a swept side fringe on the left, her hair was nearly bum-length but not quite. The girl in black jeans had brown eyes and the girl in brown jeans had blue eyes.

As they were going upstairs, the one with her hair in a ponytail turned round and started shooting bullets at the other girl. The girl dodged the bullets effectively and they hit a few of the cops behind them. The girls grinned at each other and returned to running up the stairs. They then jumped over the balcony and landed unharmed on the ground floor three floors below. The remaining cops who were chasing them took the escalators as the girls quickly took the right hallway towards the subway escalators. The cops started to catch up as the girls stood each foot on the railings either side of the escalator and slid down. One cop managed to grab the girl dressed fully in black. She looked into his eyes as hers turned golden and said:

Girl: We have done nothing wrong. You will let us go immediately.

The cop does as she says and the girls continue running. They head towards the boarding lounge. As they walk quickly through the tunnel to board the plane, someone starts shooting from underneath the tunnel. This creates a large hole and some of the passengers fall through. The girls then spot another cop. The one in black jeans approaches him and flings her arms around him. The two kiss then all three of them run on board the plane. A split second after them and a few other passengers get aboard the plane, the whole tunnel collapses. The pilot and crew were totally oblivious. The air hostess hadn't even bothered to check the tickets; she was too busy filing her nails. The three sat down together a few rows back.

Xxx

At the police station

One of the cops, whose name badge read Officer Deerin, shoved two pictures of the girls at the airport at the chief of police. He pointed to the picture of the one wearing brown jeans.

Officer Deerin: That, chief, is Lorenza Tatlioni.

He then pointed to the picture of the other girl.

Officer Deerin: And **that** is Toni Innoteya. They raided an airport recently.

Chief: I'm sure the squad has it under control.

Officer Deerin: No, they don't. They managed to escape on a plane going across the border, where we have no jurisdiction. And sources say that Officer Gerran helped them escape.

Chief: Oh no no no. This won't do at all. Where is the plane going?

Officer Deerin: The isle of Losta Soualas sir.

Chief: Losta Soualas?

Officer: It means lost souls sir.

Chief: I see. You can contact officer Gerran and tell him he's fired. And contact the local authorities of Losta Soualas. Let them know that they've got trouble headed their way.

Officer Deerin: Yes sir.

Xxx

Back on the plane

Lorenza: Ay, gracias to heaven above. I canoot believe it.

Toni: We made it. We're headed to Losta Soualas.

Gerran: We sure are.

After the plane has landed, Gerran's phone rings. He answers it.

All throughout the phone conversation, the girls can only hear Gerran's side of the conversation:

Gerran: Hello.

Officer Deerin: Chief says you're fired.

Officer Deerin hangs up. Gerran does the same and puts his phone back in his pocket.

Toni: Who was it?

Gerran: Officer Deerin. Apparently I'm fired.

Toni and Lorenza laugh at Gerran's nonchalant tone. He pretends to be annoyed for a few seconds and then gives up the charade and laughs with them.

Xxx

Chapter 2: Introductions

At their new house

They had all unpacked and Toni and Lorenza were sitting at the table, wearing their pyjamas, chatting, while Gerran was asleep. Lorenza was wearing a white short sleeved pyjama top with a yellow smiley face on it and plain white pyjama bottoms with white furry boots. Toni was wearing a pink buttoned long-sleeved top with white pyjama bottoms with roses on them and grey furry boots. Lorenza's hair was in her usual messy pony-tail and Toni also had her hair in a ponytail, but her ponytail was neat. They were doing night watch. Although they were safer here, it had become a habit and they wanted to make sure everything was secure.

Toni: Remember when we first met?

Lorenza: Ay, omia, of course I do. How on earth could I forget?

Xxx

FLASHBACK- YEAR 8 DINNER DANCE, 2008

Toni was wearing a brown halter neck dress with plain black leggings, a black leather jacket and brown, leather knee-high boots. Her hair was in its usual straight style. Lorenza was wearing a plain white t-shirt, light blue denim jeans, a blue denim jean jacket and white high-heel strappy sandals. Her hair was in its usual messy ponytail. At that moment both girls simultaneously pulled out a gun and aimed it at the unexpecting students. Toni quickly pulled another gun out and aimed it at the public and aimed the one in her right hand at Lorenza.

Toni: Now what's your business here?

Lorenza: I- I- I'm here to steal the money from the school.

Toni: Are you sure about that?

Lorenza: Um...

She nods her head meekly.

Lorenza: I don't know. I guess not. This thing doesn't even have any bullets in.

Toni: Rule number 1. Never tell anybody there aren't any bullets in your gun. You could still make people think there are and scare them into doing what you want. Here.

Lorenza looks intrigued then confused as Toni chucks her the gun she was aiming at her.

Toni: Wadya say we work together and split the profit?

Lorenza: I'd like that.

The head comes into the hall.

Toni: Ah, the head. You can go get us our money. NOW. And don't forget a single penny.

Head: Why should I? Just put the gun down.

Toni: (to Lorenza) What's your name by the way?

Lorenza: I'm Lorenza.

Toni: I'm Toni. Now aim your gun at him will you?

She nods toward the head and Lorenza does as she's told.

Toni: Now, Mr. Head. If you don't do as I ask, then this girl gets her head blown off.

She aims her gun at a random student.

Head: You wouldn't.

Toni: Oh but I would. Ask Lorenza here. She's the one training her gun on you.

Lorenza: Trust me she would. As would I.

Lorenza's confidence levels had gone up dramatically. The head was now sweating.

Head: I don't believe you'd do it.

Toni shoots the student girl in the head repeatedly until her head falls off. Some students scream and the head looks horrified.

Head: Lorenza, you won't stand by and let her do this, will you?

Lorenza targets her gun on a male student and shoots him in the head, the student falls down dead.

Lorenza: What do you think garcon?

Head: Ok, the money's in the office round the corner. Here's the key.

They grab all the money out of the office and return to the hall.

Toni: Thanks.

She shoots the head, once in the heart and he falls dead to the floor.

Toni: Buh-bye.

The girls give a little wave.

Toni: You students, we were never here, got it?

The students nod constantly.

Lorenza: Good.

The girls grin at each other.

Xxx

BACK TO PRESENT DAY, LORENZA AND TONI AT TABLE.

Toni: Good times.

Lorenza: What would I be without you?

Toni: Oh, you'd still be you, of course.

Lorenza: I wouldn't be as con-fi-dont.

Toni: Sure you would. That confidence comes from you, not from me.

Lorenza: But you helped bring it out, zo thankoo.

Toni: You're welcome.

Lorenza and Toni stand up as they hear someone knock on the door. Lorenza and Toni look at each other warily.

Lorenza: I'll get it.

Toni: Wait.

Toni looks out the window to see that at the door is a cop.

Toni: It's a cop. He's a native. We're all clear. Go.

Lorenza runs down stairs to get the door. She opens the door and smiles at the officer.

Lorenza: Good night, isn't it officer? What can I do por vous?

Officer: What are you doing up so late?

Lorenza: Oh, me and my sister are total night owls. We oh so love the night.

Officer: I see. Is your sister up?

Lorenza: Yes, she is. She is up the stairs, I can call her if you wish, no?

Officer: Yes that would be good. What are you and your sister called?

Lorenza: I'm Lori Rallut, and my sister is Taya Grant.

Officer: Your sister doesn't have the same last name as you?

Lorenza/Lori: No, she ist married to Gerran Grant. They got married only a few months ago. I call her now, yes?

Officer: Yes, that would be good.

Lorenza: TAYA!

Upstairs Toni heard the name she recognised from the fake ID'S that they had made earlier that night, being called. She quickly came down the stairs and smiled at the cop at the door.

Toni/Taya: Hi officer. Can we help you?

The officer suddenly looked at the girls suspicious.

Officer: Wait, if you two are sisters, why don't you speak with the same accent?

Lorenza/Lori: I was born in Spain...

Toni quickly got the gist.

Toni/Taya: ... And I was born in England. Our mum liked to travel a lot. She was French.

Officer: You don't sound English.

Toni/Taya: Oh really? And, do tell me officer, what does an English woman sound like?

Officer: You're right. I'm sorry ma'am.

Toni/Taya: That's alright officer.

Officer: Your sister tells me you're married.

Toni/Taya: That's correct.

Officer: Then why don't you live with your husband?

Toni/Taya: Whatever do you mean? I do live with my husband.

Officer: Then where is he? What about your sister?

Lorenza/Lori: We all live together. Gerran is upstairs asleep.

Officer: Mr Grant is asleep? Why are you girls not asleep as well then?

Lorenza: I already told you. We're night owls. We love the night.

Toni: Whereas Gerran is more of a morning and day person.

Officer: Then when do you find the time to do stuff together?

Lorenza: Well, we do sleep at night sometimes, chico.

Officer: Right. Well I was told to come here on the basis that two dangerous criminals called Toni & Lorenza were here, but my sources were obviously wrong. Sorry for bothering you girls.

Both: That's alright officer.

The Officer leaves and the girls close the door and start laughing as soon as they're sure the Officer is too far away to hear them.

Toni: Oh that was close.

Lorenza: Zoo close, if you ask me.

Toni: Ehh, meh.

They start laughing again. They walked back upstairs and resumed chatting.

Xxx

Chapter 3: First Impressions

The next day Gerran and Toni were sitting at the table drinking tea while Lorenza was out getting some supplies.

Toni: You remember the day we first met?

Gerran: Of course I do. It's not a day I'm going to forget in a hurry.

Toni: Nah, me either. Bit of a rocky start.

Gerran: (nods slightly) Yeah.

They both smile brightly at one another.

FLASHBACK: When Lorenza and Toni met Gerran.

Lorenza and Toni had just come off a plane that had just come from Hawaii. Lorenza had her hair in her usual messy ponytail and had a halo of flowers. She was wearing a bright orange Hawaiian top with brown chinos and white trainers. Toni had her hair in bunches that flowed down her back and also had a halo of flowers. Toni was wearing a white and blue checked top with pink chinos and white trainers. The girls were both laughing and both had cocktails in their hands that had little umbrella's in them. As they stepped further into the airport, they finished their drinks then threw the glasses on the floor then deliberately stepped on them so they shattered. They pocketed chocolates and souvenirs from around. They walked into the airport's McDonald's' and Lorenza discretely held a gun to the cashier's throat. The girls both smirk.

Lorenza: (whispers) Get us two large chicken nugget meals, chips and Pepsi's and a couple portions of mozzarella sticks. And make it free. Got it?

Cashier: Got it. Eat in or take away?

Lorenza: (in normal voice) Take away.

The cashier gets them their meals and Lorenza discretely puts the gun back in her pocket.

Toni: (whispers) If you tell anyone about this you're dead.

The cashier nods frantically then checks the C.T.V and his eyes widened. There was nothing but static. The girls' smirks grew wider.

Toni: (In normal voice) Thank you.

The girls take their meals and walk out and then start laughing. A cop approaches them. His nametag reads Officer G Haaren.

Officer G. Haaren: Something funny ladies?

Toni: No sir. We were just laughing at what the cashier guy who served us said.

Officer Haaren: What did he say?

Lorenza: Ay, omia, he said that... (laughs) He bet we liked romantic nights in.

Toni: (snorts) He was obviously trying his luck trying to flirt with us. And not doing a very good job.

Officer G. Haaren: Would you like me to talk to him?

Lorenza: No, that's alright thank you sir.

Officer G. Haaren: Ok then, have a good day ladies.

Toni: Thank you sir.

Just as Officer Haaren is about to leave, another officer comes round the corner. His nametag read Officer Hallen G.

Officer Hallen: Officer Haaren, there you are. A cashier has just reported that two girls held a gun to him and threatened to shoot him if he didn't give them their meals free.

Officer Haaren: Girls you've just come out of McDonalds. Do you have a receipt?

Toni hands him their receipt.

Officer Haaren: Ok it's legit. Did you girls see anything? Or hear something maybe?

Lorenza: No sir, I'm afraid we did not.

Officer Haaren: Ok, goodbye girls.

Toni: Goodbye Officer.

Officer Haaren walks away and Officer Hallen looks deep in thought.

Officer Hallen: Come with me, girls.

Toni: Why sir?

Officer Hallen: To sort this entire thing out.

Toni and Lorenza have worried looks on their faces.

Lorenza: Are we in ztrouble?

Officer Hallen: Well girls, we'll have to see about that.

Officer Hallen walks the two in to McDonald's and walks them up to the cashier who is waving frantically at him.

Officer Hallen: Are these the two girls you described?

Cashier: Y-yes that's them.

Toni glares at him and mouths 'I warned you', without Officer Hallen seeing.

Officer Hallen: Ok. I'll deal with them accordingly.

While Officer Hallen isn't looking Toni texts Lorenza 'I have a feeling we're not gonna get away with this one'. Lorenza texts back 'me too'. They put their phones away as Officer Hallen turns round. Officer Hallen then takes them out of McDonalds and brings them to a secluded room not too far away that is located in the airport. They sit down on the chairs and pop a chewing gum in their mouth each out of nervousness.

Officer Hallen: Well girls. Armed shoplifting. That's a serious crime. I'm gonna have to bring you in. (As Lorenza opens her mouth to speak) Don't even try lying to me.

Toni: I can see you're a man of integrity. I respect that. Y'know we know a lot of members of your police force, and none of them are anything like you. You're different. You have certain air to you.

Officer Hallen: Oh? And how come you've met all these officers?

Toni: We've simply been at the wrong place at the wrong time.

Officer Hallen: I've told you before. Don't lie to me.

Toni: I'm not lying, Mr Hallen. I'm simply saying that the statement is true for times before this one.

Officer Hallen: I find that hard to believe. And call me Gerran. Mr. Hallen doesn't suit me.

Toni smirks as Lorenza looks between the two, raising her eyebrows in suspicion.

Toni: Oh? Is that your first name?

Gerran: No, actually. It's my last name. Hallen is my first name. But, like I said, it doesn't suit me.

Toni: I see.

Gerran: And if you're trying to distract me, it's not working. I am *very* focused.

Lorenza (muttering) + Toni (clear): I can see that.

Lorenza: (mumbling) never gonna let us go. This stinks.

Toni sends her a glare, which softens when she sees her face. She mouths:' we'll be ok'. Lorenza doesn't look too sure about this but mouths back 'If you're sure.' Toni mouths back: 'I am'. Officer Gerran clears his throat.

Gerran: Am I interrupting something.

Lorenza: Not at all.

Gerran: Good, now back to business. I'm taking you downtown.

The girls' eyes widen.

Both: What? But-(sighs)

Xxx

Chapter 4: Maximum Security

Officer Hallen leads them to a prison upstate and throws them in a holding cell. After he leaves the girls check for CCTV and thoroughly but discretely disable all security cameras.

Toni: Ok. We're clear here. Now we need to think of a plan. First step is to get to the main security office and disable all cameras, CCTV and defence systems. We also need to deal with any guards on patrol.

Lorenza looks at Toni sceptically.

Lorenza: You're crazy. I knew I shouldn't have got involved with you.

Toni: Yeah? Well, you did. So... Yeah.

Lorenza: Maybe we should jusst calls it quits. Serve time and get out on good behaviour.

It was Toni's turn to eye Lorenza sceptically.

Toni: Now you're the one who's talkin' crazy. Y'know what they do to you in prison? They beat you and torture you to point of the death. Anyone who's bigger or stronger than you will grind you to a pulp. Guards *and* Prisoners.

Lorenza looked down frightened.

Lorenza: I'm scared.

Toni: Use it. But don't show it. In prison, being scared is a weakness.

Lorenza: You talk like you've been in prison?

Toni: Nope. But I've talked to a man who knows. Someone who was in a high security prison, like this one.

Lorenza: I see.

Toni came and sat opposite her.

Toni: Lorenza... It'll be ok, I promise. We're gonna get out of here.

Xxx

Two weeks passed and they devised a plan. Today was the day they were going to go through with it. So far they had kept their heads down and avoided any fights or thugs. That was until one came up to them. His name badge, they had been forced to wear name badges, read Henry Heinrik. He was one of the leaders of one of the top gangs in this prison.

Henry: Toni and Lorenza.

He read their name badges.

Henry: What did you guys do?

Toni: We got free meals from MacDonald's by holding the cashier at gunpoint.

Henry: (laughs) Pathetic.

He spat. Lorenza looked him in the eyes seeming confident but not feeling it. Henry pulled Toni out of her cell and shoved her against the wall.

Henry: Fight with me girly.

Toni: Gladly. If you make the first move.

She smirked slightly and he raised an eyebrow.

Henry: And why do I have to make the first move?

Toni: That way I can't be held responsible for my actions. I would be merely defending myself from a criminal thug and I wouldn't get into trouble for it, you would.

Henry eyed her up and down as if seeing her for the first time.

Henry: Smart girl.

He threw a punch and she caught it in the palm of her hand and switched their positions so he was against the wall. He pushed her over with the other hand and she fell. She quickly rolled into a standing position. He threw another punch and she ducked and tripped him. He fell and struggled to get back up. That was when Officer Gerran chose to walk down the hallway. Great (!) She thought. Perfect timing (!) Henry got up and forcefully pushed her over with all his might landing on top of her and preventing her from getting up. She struggled against him but it was no use. She punched him hard in the face knocking him unconscious. His body sagged and she still struggled to push him off her. Officer Gerran came up to her and helped pushed him off her. She breathed a sigh of relief.

Toni: Thank you.

She lay on the floor for a minute gasping for breath. Lorenza sat on her bed looking shocked. Gerran nodded and lifted her up and placed her on her bed.

Gerran: Rest. You'll need it.

Xxx

As soon as it was lights out Lorenza and Toni sprung out of bed ready for action.

Lorenza: Let’s do this thing.

Toni nodded. They tiptoe ran down the hallway desperately trying not to make any noise. They avoided the cameras and got to the main control room. There was a guard outside the door.

Toni: Shoot. What are we going to do?

Lorenza looked around thinking. She saw a knife lying on the ground next to her. She picked it up and threw it down the corridor then quickly hid again. The guard saw the knife and ran down the hallway. Toni snuck up behind him and knocked him out then nodded to Lorenza. They entered the control room. Toni took out a bottle of knock-out spray she had stolen from one of the guards. She sprayed it into the room, knocking the guards in there out. Lorenza sat at the controls turning off the cameras, CCTV and defences. She nodded signalling Toni, who was on guard. The two quickly left the room. They walked to the main door, using the knock out spray on the guards there. They ran out onto the yard where they saw dogs.

Both: Holy shit.

They sprayed the knock out gas but the knock out gas only worked on humans. It didn't work on dogs. Lorenza took a dog whistle out of her pocket and whistled a lullaby on it, sending the dogs to sleep.

Toni: (whispers) How did you do that?

Lorenza shrugs slightly, smiling.

Lorenza: (whispers) I have many talents.

Toni smiled back at her. The two ran further into the distance until they came across a barbed wire fence. It looked as if it could be electric.

Toni: It's electric.

Lorenza saw a small gap under a part of the fence.

Lorenza: There's a gap right there. But whether we get through it without touching the fence or not is a different question.

Toni nodded slightly.

Toni: Ok. You go first.

Lorenza starts to head under the gap when Toni pulls out a pair of wire cutters with rubber handles.

Lorenza: Where did you get those?

Toni: You'd be surprised what you find in prison.

Toni cuts the barbed wire and they stepped through it and keep running. They reach the main gate which requires a password to get through.

Toni: Oh shit. What do you think the password is?

Lorenza: I have no idea.

They both thought about it. They didn't know what it could be and they didn't know who owned the prison.

Toni: Oh. A clue would be really helpful right now.

Gate: Clue: Tis a song that can be made by something that flies and lives in trees.

They both stare at the gate in shock.

Lorenza: Ok. So what could that mean?

Toni: I have no idea.

They both pondered it for a while when a light bulb lit up over Toni's head.

Toni: ooh I know. The answer is... A Song-Bird.

Gate: That is correct.

The gate opens and they look at each other, squealing excitedly. They quickly run through the gate. It closes after they have gone through it. They hop into a Mercedes that had had the window down and drive away in it. Free. Toni grinned at Lorenza.

Toni: First stop. Airport MacDonald's. We have some unfinished business.

Lorenza rolls her eyes.

Lorenza: Oh Toni.

Xxx

AT MACDONALD'S

They walked in looking for the cashier that had served them. He was behind the counter. MacDonald's was just closing. All the other staff had gone home. Toni pulled a gun out of her pocket and aimed it at him.

Cashier: Please. Don't.

Toni: Can't say I didn't warn you.

She shoots him in the heart twice and he falls down dead. The girls quickly, but sneakily, come out of MacDonald's and head out of the airport in their new Mercedes.

End of flashback

Gerran: So *that's* how you escaped. I always wondered about that.

Toni: (laughs embarrassedly) Yeah.

Gerran tucks a stray hair behind her ear, staring into her eyes lovingly. Their hands unconsciously entwine together on the table.

Toni: It took a while for us to fall for each other though.

Gerran: And even longer to say those three little words.

They both laugh.

Gerran: We were young and stupid and naive. It took time to come to our senses.

Toni: It sure did. But now, I couldn't be without you.

Gerran: Nor could I you.

Xxx

Chapter 5: Flashbacks

*Flashbacks- 1st flashback- Scotland Cineworld and KFC.

Toni and Lorenza had snuck in to the upstairs cinema in Scotland Cineworld. They had recently departed from England. They couldn't stay there because of their criminal record. Damn that Officer Hallen Gerran. They had sneaked a pick a mix in and had faked their cinema tickets. They hadn't needed them because nobody had checked if they had any. The movie they were watching was 'Marley & Me'. At the end of the movie, both girls cried like crazy.

Toni: (Teary) That poor little doggy.

Lorenza: Yeah. It's so sad.

Toni spots Officer Gerran at the doorway and quickly ducks down slightly so he can't see her.

Toni: (Whispers) Lorenza. Get down. Officer Gerran is in the cinema.

Lorenza: What?

Lorenza looks around and then spots him in the doorway talking to the theatre assistant.

Lorenza: (Whispers) Oh my god.

She quickly ducked down out of sight. The movie finished and the credits had stopped rolling. They needed to get out of the cinema. But officer Gerran was blocking the exit. Toni looked around and spotted the in-theatre toilets.

Toni: Quick. To the toilets.

Lorenza nodded and the girls ran into the toilets, undetected. They waited a few minutes and then peeked out. Officer Gerran had gone. They quickly exited the cinema and ran over to KFC. They walked over to the counter and ordered. They handed over the money. They couldn't get in trouble with Officer Gerran so nearby.

Counter worker: This is counterfeit money.

The girls looked over the counter and could see a clear yellow line over the bills.

Toni: It is? Maybe you used the wrong pen?

Counter Worker: No I used the right one. Just hand over real money and its fine.

Lorenza: We don't have any other money.

Toni and Lorenza looked frantic. It was all a façade but hey. They had real money, but they didn't like to use it unless absolutely necessary.

Counter worker: Right. Well where did you get the money from?

Toni: It's change from Cineworld.

Counter worker: I see. Well I'll call the police and see if we can get this all sorted out.

Lorenza: No! You don't need to do that.

Toni: Let me double check my purse.

The counter worker reached over and put a hand on Toni's to stop her searching.

Counter Worker: It's not just about the money. Cineworld have committed a serious felony.

Toni: Honestly. Don't worry about it. Ah. Here we go.

She pulled a twenty out of her purse and handed it over. The counter worker took it and they sat down to eat their meal. While they did, the counter worker phoned the police. The girls noticed Officer Gerran come in the door and kept their heads down. Officer Gerran and the counter worker discussed the whole counterfeit money incident.

Counter worker: These girls have been given fake money and deserve to get it back. Cineworld has stolen from them.

The counter worker pointed over to Toni & Lorenza.

Officer Gerran: I have a feeling they're lying.

He walked over to them and took a seat next to Toni, their hips touching.

Officer Gerran: Hi girls.

Both: Hi.

Officer Gerran: Long time, no see. Aren't you supposed to be in prison?

Toni: Well... Yeah. Pretty much.

Lorenza: But we never do what we're supposed to do. I really hate you, Toni.

Toni: What did I do?

Lorenza: You bought me into this life. I never wanted it.

Toni: Oh come on. We've had great adventures together. And besides. You were the one who decided to raid that school at gunpoint. That was you. On your own.

Lorenza: You decided to do the same.

Toni: But I didn't help you with your decision. We met after that. You made that decision yourself.

Lorenza: Yess? Well, I wish I never had. Then I would never have met you and I wouldn't be in this mess.

Toni watches as Lorenza runs out the door.

Toni: Lorenza! Lorenza. Lorenza... (Sighs defeatedly)

Tears start rolling down her cheeks and she faces Gerran.

Toni: Y'know what? Just bloody well kill me already. She's right. She's always right. I'm nothing. I stand for nothing.

Gerran: Maybe you should resolve your ways.

Toni: (scoffs) As if. Maybe you should resolve your ways.

Gerran: I haven't done anything wrong.

Toni: Exactly. You should try walking on the wild side once in a while.

Gerran: I don't think so. I'm a highly trained officer. That's not what I do.

Toni: Whatevs. I can't believe she left. I need her back.

She sobs harder and Gerran pulls her into his chest.

Gerran: It'll be okay. Look...I... I'll tell you what. I'll take away your sentence. Wipe your slate clean for everything you've done until now.

Toni: Really?

Gerran: Really?

Toni: (teary) Thank you so much.

Gerran: But I can't promise anything for future crimes.

Toni nods slightly.

Gerran: Go find your friend.

Toni nods again and goes off to find Lorenza. She gets in her Mercedes and goes off to find her friend. She noticed that Lorenza had taken the blue ford focus to leave in. She drove and drove and drove, until eventually she saw Lorenza walking into a garden centre. She quickly parked and then ran after her. She reached her and tapped her on the shoulder. Lorenza turned around.

Lorenza: Toni. I'm sorry I left you there to get caught. We're supposed to be in this together.

Toni: I'm sorry too. If you want, you can go and live a normal life and get away from all this crime.

Lorenza: But will you?

Toni shook her head slightly.

Toni: I don't think so. It's all I know.

Lorenza: Well in that case... We're in it together.

Lorenza and Toni smile at each other and pull into a hug.

Lorenza: How'd you get past Officer Gerran?

Toni: He took pity on me or something, I guess. He's dropped all of our charges.

Lorenza: Really?

Toni: Really. So let's not get caught ever again.

Xxx

Back to present day

Toni: And we never did.

Gerran: true. Even I couldn't stop you after that point.

Xxx

2nd flashback

Toni and Lorenza bumped into Gerran in a shopping mall. Toni was trying on a dress and came out of the changing room to show it off. Gerran eyed her up and down, admiring her body. She looked beautiful in it. She was beautiful. She spotted him and waved smiling. He smiled and waved back. He walked over to them.

Lorenza: You look abs fabooloos, Toni.

Toni: Thanks Lor.

Gerran: Yeah. You look gorgeous.

Toni blushes.

Toni: Thank you…

The two stare deeply into each other’s eyes and Lorenza eyes them suspiciously. The two kiss. Gerran picks her up, deepening the kiss. She wraps her legs around his waist. He feels her against him and goes hard. He puts her down.

Gerran: I-

With that, he runs off.

Toni: Gerran!

She sighs and runs into the changing room to get changed. She quickly but sneakily places the dress in her bag with all security tags taken off, and runs after him. Lorenza sighs and runs after her.

Lorenza: What waz zthat all about?

Toni: I think I've fallen for him.

Lorenza: Oh.

They found Gerran sitting on a bench outside. Toni places a hand on his shoulder and sits next to him.

Toni: Gerran, you ok?

He looks over to her. He notices that she is now wearing red skinny jeans, black and white trainers and a brown tank top with a black leather jacket. Her hair is straight, flowing down her back.

Gerran: I'm fine.

He looks away. She turns his head to face her.

Toni: look at me when I'm talking to you.

He reluctantly faces her, his eyes not willing to make eye contact. She cupped his face in her hands, stroking his cheeks, and smiling softly. She leans in for a kiss. The kiss is passionate and heated and loving. His hand rubs up and down her thigh and the kiss breaks off as they pull away.

Gerran: Screw it. That's my cop career down the drain.

She smiled again.

Toni: Maybe not.

He smiled back and their hands linked. They were finally together.

Xxx

3rd flashback: Those three little words

Lorenza, Toni and Gerran were in a bank being held hostage. Toni and Lorenza found this ironic as usually it was them holding people hostage. There were loads of armed robbers, too many for them to take. They heard another gunshot and another scream. Toni flinched. Her hand clamped down tighter on Gerran's.

Lorenza: Toni. If we don't make it out of here, just know, you'll always be my best friend.

Toni smiled sweetly at Lorenza.

Toni: And you'll always be mine.

She looked over to Gerran, their hands entwined and their eyes locked.

Both: I love you.

The couple shared an intimate kiss. Toni flinched again as she heard another gunshot and another scream. She stood up and walked out of their hiding place.

Lorenza: Toni, where are you going?

Toni: Someone's gotta stop this. Or we're all gonna die here anyway. Lorenza, if we can manage to not get caught for like a billions crimes, raid airports, and escape a max high security prison, then we can face this.

Lorenza stood up and held Toni's hand, letting her know that she was with her every step of the way. Gerran also stood up.

Gerran: Well, I may not have done any of that, but... I was the only cop to ever capture the two most dangerous criminals in the world.

Toni and Lorenza smiled mischievously at him.

Lorenza: That you were.

The three head into the main room, ducking, tucking and rolling to avoid the bullets. Toni kicked down a few of the robbers and took one of their guns. She aimed it at the other robbers. They aimed their guns at her. Toni motioned for Gerran and Lorenza to attack. Lorenza rolled forward and tripped a few of the robbers up. Toni shot a few and Gerran handcuffed some to posts. It took a long time and it was a tiring and extremely long battle, but eventually it was over and they had won.

Toni: Let's get out of here guys. I'm sick of this place.

Both: Agreed.

Toni took some money from the banks and the trio walked out of the door and drove away in the Mercedes.

Xxx

4th flashback: The proposal

Gerran came into Toni's room. Toni was in her underwear, brushing her hair. She saw Gerran and put the hairbrush down at the serious look on Gerran's face.

Toni: Something up?

Gerran got down on one knee and Toni gasped, her eyes widening in shock.

Gerran: Toni. You are everything to me. I know I don't show it well or say it that often, but I love you. With all my heart. It would be the greatest honour and you'd make me the happiest man alive. Please.

He pulls a ring box out of his pocket and opens it to reveal a beautiful diamond engagement ring. Toni gasps again, making it sound more like a soft squeal.

Gerran: Will you marry me?

Toni jumps up and down in excitement and squeals excitedly.

Toni: Yes, yes, yes!

Gerran stands up and delicately places the ring on her finger. After he has done so, she throws herself at him, wrapping her legs around his waist. He catches her and they kiss passionately.

Toni: Mrs Hallen Gerran. I like the sound of that.

Gerran grins at her.

Gerran: As do I.

They fall back onto the bed.

Xxx

5th flashback: The wedding

Gerran was standing at the aisle, waiting for his bride. He saw bridesmaid Lorenza coming down the aisle sprinkling flowers everywhere. Toni followed behind her in a beautiful white and puffy Armani wedding dress. There were flowers in her hair and a bouquet of flowers in her hand, and she looked absolutely stunning. She joined them and held Gerran's hand. There weren't actually people here as this wedding had to be kept secret. They looked deep into each other's eyes and said their vows. They kissed and were pronounced husband and wife.

Xxx

Back to present day

Toni: Happy times.

Gerran: Yup. I love you Mrs Gerran.

Toni: I love you too Gerran.

Xxx

Chapter 6: The end of an era

Toni, Lorenza and Gerran were walking down the street when some police officers were walking towards them. They relaxed when they saw the police officers walk past. Lorenza collapsed to the floor and Toni and Gerran were instantly by her side.

Toni: Lorenza? What's wrong?

They noticed Lorenza shaking and her arm twitching. They notice her breath is jagged and her chest is tight.

Toni: I think she's having a heart attack. Call an ambulance!

Gerran quickly calls an ambulance, stunned and at loss for words. The ambulance comes five minutes later. The paramedic rushes to Lorenza's pulse and heartbeat. He shakes his head. Toni and Gerran look to him worriedly.

Paramedic: I'm sorry. She's dead.

Toni: (screams and cries) No! She can't be dead. She can't be. (softly) Lorenza...

Tears also flow down Gerran's face. He wraps his arms around Toni and brings her into his chest to comfort her. They both watch and cry as the paramedic put Lorenza in a body bag and take her away.

Xxx

A few days later and Gerran and Toni were walking down the street, when they accidentally turned into a dead end. They were suddenly surrounded by English police officers. The officers held them at gunpoint.

Officer: Get ready to die. Can't wait to be rid of you two. Where's your friend?

Toni: (spitefully) She's dead.

Officer: Less work for us then.

Gerran: (spits) You monster.

Officer: No different than you.

Toni: Gerran...

Gerran: Yeah?

Toni: I just want you to know... if we die here...

Toni: I'm pregnant.

Gerran looks at her shocked.

Gerran: You are?

Toni nods and Gerran smiles at her, placing a hand on her stomach. The officers don't notice this. The officers start firing and a bullet hits Gerran. He falls down dead.

Toni (screams) No!

She drops down beside him, cradling his head. She puts his hand to her stomach.

Toni: We love you, Gerran. Forever and always.

Toni looks up to the officers and then back down at Gerran.

Toni: That's it. I'm out. I can't take this anymore. This life has cost me everything I hold dear. I need to start fresh. But I'll never forget.

The officers look at her confused but still aim their guns at her.

Toni: If you're gonna kill me fine. But kill me after nine months.

Officer: Why?

Toni: Because I'm pregnant doofus.

Officer: Oh. I see. Were you serious about starting fresh?

Toni: Completely. No more life of crime for me. I wanna start new, change my name. Again.

The officer nodded but still kept their guns trained on her.

Officer: I'm afraid we can't let you go.

She nodded and took her gun from her pocket and trained it on one of the officers.

Toni: Then I'm sorry.

She quickly shot the officers one by one in quick succession, avoiding any bullets that came her way. She then ran off into the distance. She went home, packed up her stuff and drove away to start her new life. She rubbed her stomach.

Toni: Just you and me now little one. But if the angels were to ever find out you existed... Human/Angel relationships aren't permitted, let alone half angel, half human children. Looks like I'm on the run again.

Her white wings came into full view. She was once again on the run. But this time instead of from the law, it was from angels.

www.ingramcontent.com/pod-product-compliance
Ingram Content Group UK Ltd.
Pitfield, Milton Keynes, MK11 3LW, UK
UKHW020228250726
13967UKWH00001B/251